KU-634-281

MATISSE'S
MAGICAL TRAIL

Tim Hopgood   Sam Boughton

OXFORD
UNIVERSITY PRESS

For Matisse,
the world outside
his shell was a big,
scary place.

MATISSE'S
MAGICAL TRAIL

WALTHAM FOREST LIBRARIES

904 000 00640432

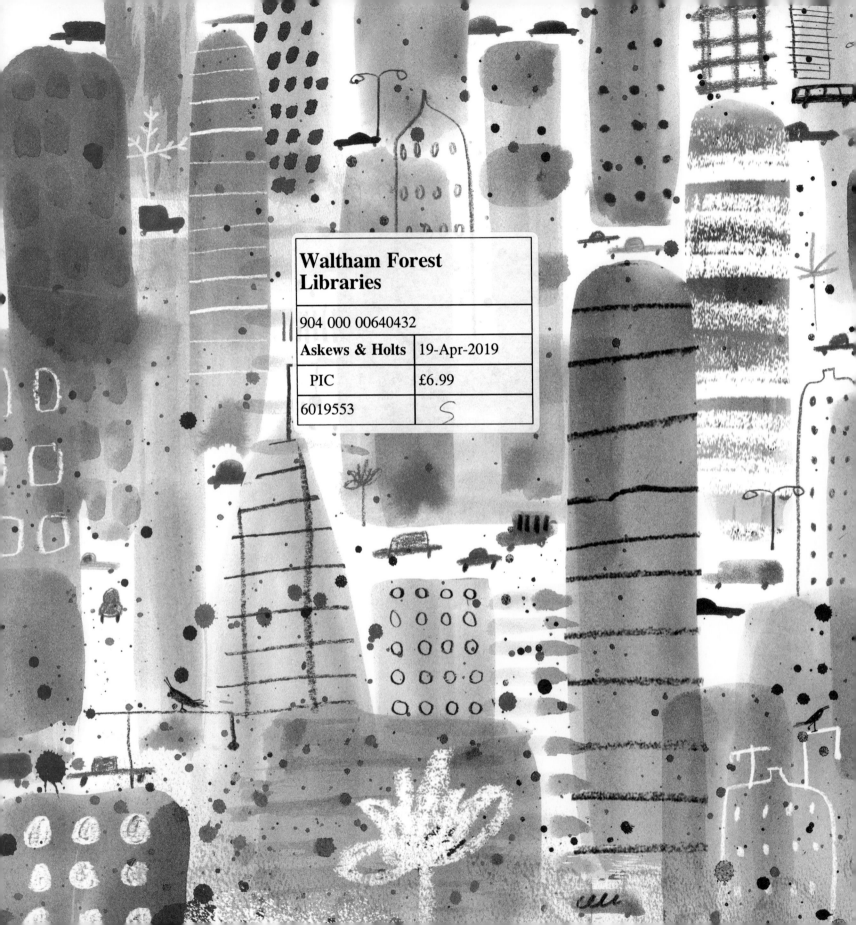

Waltham Forest Libraries

904 000 00640432	
Askews & Holts	19-Apr-2019
PIC	£6.99
6019553	

Much of his time was spent avoiding getting under people's feet!

But at night, when the streets were empty,
Matisse did what he loved most. He drew!

His drawings were like
tiny works of art.

It was a pity then that no one ever noticed them.

One moonlit night, Matisse
found himself in a quiet
spot in the heart of the city.

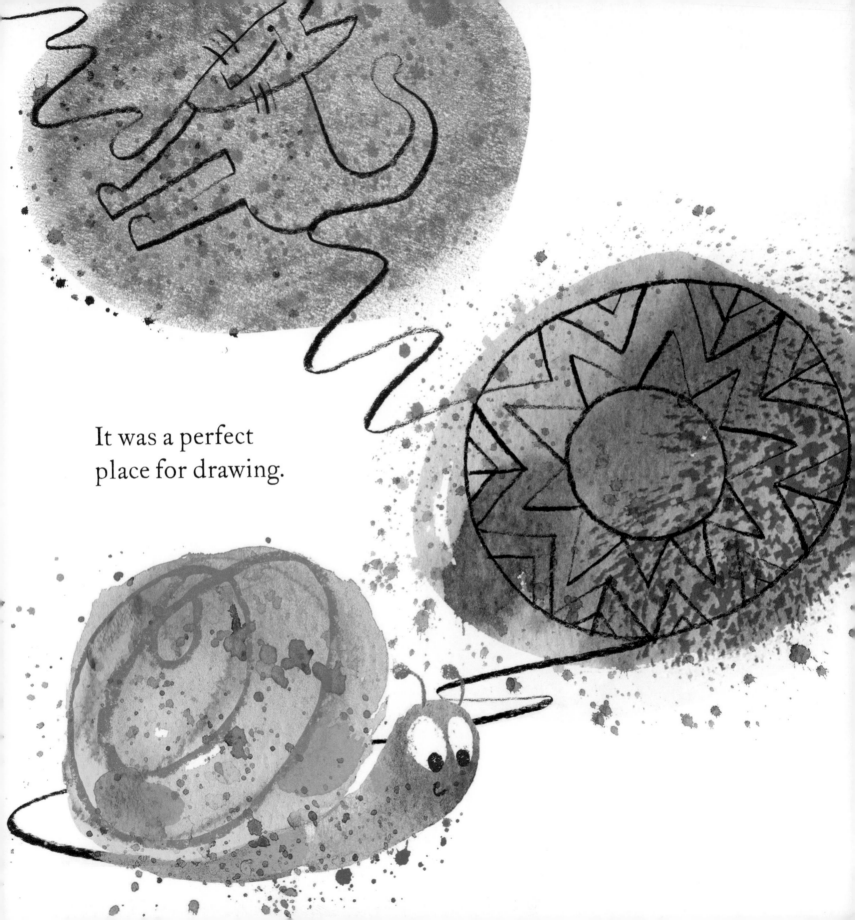

It was a perfect
place for drawing.

Perfect, at least, until morning.

Matisse hid in his shell.
He wondered if anyone
here might notice
his drawings.

A small hand picked up the
pebble with a sun on it.

Then the small hand
made the sun smile.

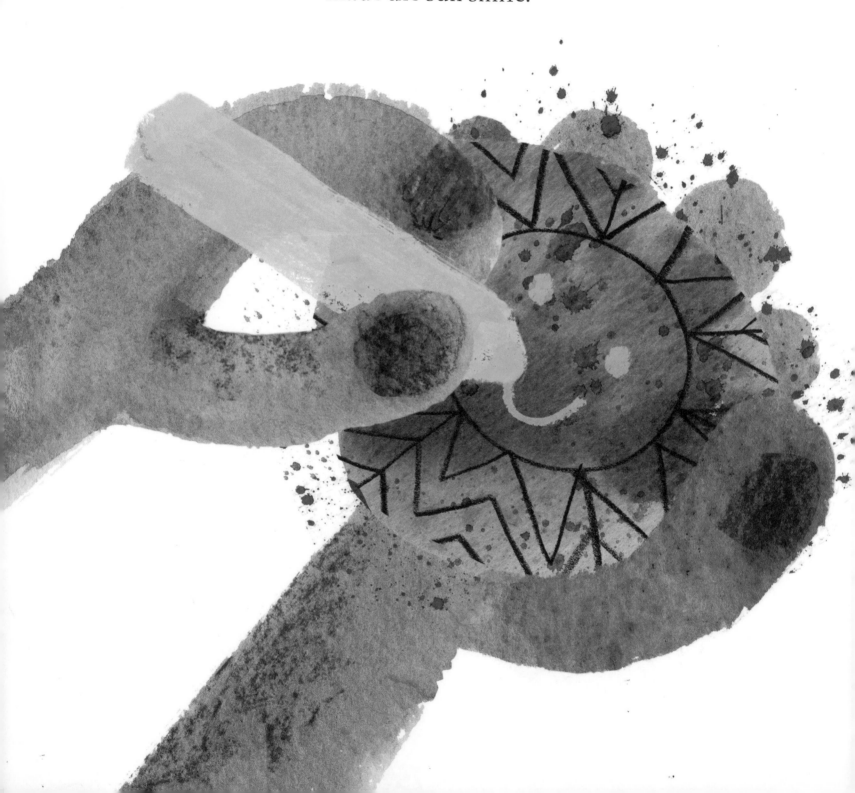

'Hello, I'm Leo,' said the boy.

And Matisse smiled back!

Leo showed Matisse's drawings to his friends.
They wanted to know where they had come from.

But Matisse was feeling shy.
He was nowhere to be seen.

'I have a plan,'
announced Leo.

The friends found more pebbles
for Matisse to draw on . . .

. . . and not just pebbles!

Later, when everyone had
disappeared, Matisse started
to draw.

By morning, he had created a trail.

A very
ARTISTIC trail.

Mrs Gray came over to
see what everyone was
looking at.

It was Leo who pointed
to Matisse on the
school wall.

Mrs Gray was astonished.
But seeing Matisse's drawings
had given her an idea . . .

. . . a very ARTISTIC idea.

Matisse was filled with joy
as the children filled the wall
with colour.

And the children
didn't stop there . . .

WOW!

The school was a magical sight.
Everyone who saw it couldn't
help but STOP and SMILE.

And who would have believed that it all started with one tiny snail?

That night, realising that the world
is full of walls that could all be made
beautiful, Matisse decided it was time
to move on.

But not before doing one
last drawing . . .

...especially for Leo
and his friends.

I wonder where Matisse is heading next? If you're lucky, you never know, you might spot him on a wall near you!

For Patrick Brill (AKA the artist Bob and
Roberta Smith) – T.H.

For budding Matisses everywhere – S.B.

OXFORD
UNIVERSITY PRESS

Great Clarendon Street, Oxford OX2 6DP
Oxford University Press is a department of the University of Oxford.
It furthers the University's objective of excellence in research, scholarship,
and education by publishing worldwide. Oxford is a registered trade mark of
Oxford University Press in the UK and in certain other countries

Text copyright © Tim Hopgood 2019
Illustrations © Sam Boughton 2019
The moral rights of the author and illustrator have been asserted
Database right Oxford University Press (maker)
First published 2019

All rights reserved. No part of this publication may be reproduced,
stored in a retrieval system, or transmitted, in any form or by any means,
without the prior permission in writing of Oxford University Press,
or as expressly permitted by law, or under terms agreed with the appropriate
reprographics rights organization. Enquiries concerning reproduction
outside the scope of the above should be sent to the Rights Department,

Oxford University Press, at the address above
You must not circulate this book in any other binding or cover
and you must impose this same condition on any acquirer

British Library Cataloguing in Publication Data

Data available
ISBN: 978-0-19-2767264

1 3 5 7 9 10 8 6 4 2

Printed in China

Paper used in the production of this book is a natural,
recyclable product made from wood grown in sustainable forests.
The manufacturing process conforms to the environmental
regulations of the country of origin.